ANNA
ANGRYSAURUS

Published in paperback in 2015 by
Wayland

Text copyright © Brian Moses
Illustrations copyright © Mike Gordon

Wayland
338 Euston Road
London NW1 3BH

Wayland Australia
Level 17/207 Kent Street
Sydney, NSW 2000

Senior editor: Victoria Brooker
Creative design: Basement68
Digital colour: Molly Hahn

British Library Cataloguing
in Publication Data:

Moses, Brian, 1950-
   Anna Angrysaurus. --
     (Dinosaurs have feelings, too)
   1. Children's stories--Pictorial
     works.
   I. Title II. Series III. Gordon, Mike,
     1948 Mar. 16-
     823.9'2-dc23
ISBN: 978 0 7502 8021 1

Printed in China
10 9 8 7 6 5 4 3 2 1

Wayland is a division of
Hachette Children's Books,
an Hachette UK company.
www.hachette.co.uk

ANNA
ANGRYSAURUS

Written by

Brian Moses

Illustrated by

Mike Gordon

WAYLAND

Anna Angrysaurus always seemed
to be angry about something.

Sometimes she got angry when she couldn't watch her favourite programme on television. "Why do we have to watch a silly tailball game? I hate tailball."

Sometimes she got angry when her brother or sister received a present and she didn't.

"But Anna, you had a present last week when you did well at school," her mum said.

Sometimes she got angry when her brother won a game of 'Who can stick their head in a T. Rex's mouth?'

"But Anna, you win that game most times.
It's good for your brother if he
wins occasionally."

Sometimes she got angry and nobody knew why she was angry. Even Anna didn't seem to know why she was angry.

When that happened she often charged at the door.

Later she felt sorry because it made her look rather silly!

Anna often ROARED or HOWLED when she was angry.

Sometimes she ROARED so loudly that the windows rattled and vases fell from shelves.

Or Anna would stamp her feet when she was angry and cause wavy lines to appear on the television.

"I wish you wouldn't do that," her dad called out. "I'm trying to watch the Dinoworld News."

"I am sorry," Anna said. 'But when I get really angry, I can't stop myself."

"I feel just like one of the volcanoes that we can see from our windows. I know I'm ready to explode."

"Anna, sometimes the things you forget to do make me angry," her mum said. "I'm thinking about when you spill your play paints on the carpet and leave me to clear up the mess."

"But I try to stay calm by counting to ten or
by taking deep breaths before I say anything.
I don't charge at the door."

"And it makes me angry," said Anna's dad, "when you and your brother and sister can't play together without calling each other silly names."

"But it helps me calm down
if I count to ten before telling
you to stop."

"Next time you start to feel angry," Anna's mum told her, "try closing your eyes and counting to five. That might help."

"Or think about the things you do well or enjoy. That might help you forget your angry feelings."

"You could also try talking to us about why you get so angry," her mum said.

"I used to lose my temper a lot when I was a young dinosaur," her dad said. "I do know how you feel."

So the next time Anna felt as if she was
a pterodactyl egg about to crack open, or
a balloon about to burst, she stopped, thought
for a bit, and then roared...

...but much
more quietly
than usual.

"That's much better," her dad said.
"Maybe now we can get a new front door."

NOTES FOR PARENTS AND TEACHERS

Read the book with children either individually or in groups.
Talk to them about what makes them angry. How do they feel
when they are angry? Do they recognise any of the things that
make Anna angry?

How would they picture themselves getting angry? Would it be
an erupting volcano, a charging bull or something else?
Perhaps they can draw how they picture themselves.

Help children to compose short poems that focus on their
own angry feelings:

> I feel angry when my brother is given sweets and I don't get any.
> I feel angry when somebody treads on my toe and doesn't
> say sorry.
> I feel angry when I break a favourite toy.
> I feel angry...

Ask children if there are some things that made them angry that
they realised afterwards weren't worth getting angry about?
How did they feel when they had calmed down and looked back
on what made them angry?

There are strategies in this book for helping children to control their
anger. Can they identify what these are? How effective do the
children think they would be? Do children have their own ways
of calming themselves down?

For example:

> I imagine myself as a balloon and then suddenly the air whooshes out.
> I imagine myself as a storm that gradually fades away.
> I imagine myself as a raging river that calms down to a gentle flow.

Look at other words and phrases for angry - cross, furious, snarl, snap, fume, rage, losing your temper, getting in a paddy, having a tantrum, throwing a wobbly, hopping mad. Ask children to write short sentences that include these words and phrases.

Sometimes children's behaviour can make other people angry. Ask them to think about what would make parents angry? What would make teachers angry? Can children think of recent examples where their own behaviour has made someone else angry?

Talk about how the actions of thoughtless people can affect others - a dog cutting its paw on broken glass, litter left around in the countryside. Are these the sort of things that could make someone angry?

Explore the notion of anger further through the sharing of picture books mentioned in the book list.

BOOKS TO SHARE

I Feel Angry by Brian Moses and Mike Gordon (Wayland)
Looking at angry feelings in an amusing yet reassuring way.

I Have Feelings by Jana Novotny Hunter, illustrated by
Sue Porter (Frances Lincoln)
Explores a whole range of feelings including angry ones.
Small children will love the little star of the book.

The Bad-Tempered Ladybird by Eric Carle (Picture Puffin)
The bad-tempered ladybird thinks that it is bigger and better
than anyone else.

Silly School by Marie-Louise Fitzpatrick (Frances Lincoln)
Beth doesn't want to go to silly school! She doesn't want
storytime, painting or singing. So what does she want to do?

The Tiger Who Was Angry by Rachel Elliot
and John Bendall-Brunello (QED Publishing)
Tiger brags about how he'll win the
jungle race, then shouts and loses
his temper with the other animals
when they don't take it seriously.
Read how he overcomes his anger.